Josh's Story

SELMA P. VERDE

AUTHOR NOTE

This story is based on characters and storyline from *The Way Series*, a coming-of-age young adult novel series about the challenges teens face. It not only provides some backstory for the series, but also presents the side of bullying we don't typically see: the perspective of the one who bullies. This is a stand-alone story, but fits well between book two, *Shawn's Way*, and book three, *The Street's Way*, as far as the storyline goes.

SELMA P. VERDE

To teens who find themselves on either side of a bullying situation. Hopefully we can start talking about the issues that cause it before it starts...

INTRODUCTION

This is a story about a teenager who bullies.

Normally, we hear this story from the perspective of the target of a bully. Not this time. In "Josh's Story," we are going to look at what happened from the one who bullies' point of view. We will start with a little background about the one who bullies. In this case, his name is Josh Alberts, an all-star baseball player who got himself into big trouble and was sent to Creekside, a juvenile detention center. After serving almost a year there, he finally started to feel some remorse for what happened, but then he received some bad news. This news is what made him mad and decided to take out his anger on his target, a character named Shawn Townson.

Our narrator is Monica Freberg, an English and social studies teacher at Brooklyn Heights High School. She takes an interest in what happened in this situation and decides to talk to both sides. She will tell the story of what happened between Josh Alberts and Shawn Townson from her point of view, using their own words.

I could hear the clicking of my heels as I walked down the hallway to my classroom. I grasped a bright pink mug of tea in my hands, one which had been a gift from one of my students. Bringing the mug up to my nose, the scent of peppermint reminded me of the chocolate peppermint cookies Grandma made for me at Christmastime. Turning the corner, I glanced at the dark red lockers that lined both sides of the hallway. The color reminded me of the cranberries which were always on the table at Thanksgiving. Since talking to my mom yesterday, family seemed to be on my mind.

There were a couple students standing by open lockers, but it was early and it was summer, so not many were at school yet. As I got closer to my classroom, I felt an early summer breeze coming through an open window and it made me smile. The scent of fresh-cut grass reminded me of the fact the baseball fields were being prepared for a game later today.

After taking a sip of tea, I walked into my classroom and set the warm cup down on my desk. It was my second year teaching summer school, and knowing how hard it is to be in school during the summer, my goal was to keep the content light but meet the requirements for all my students to get their English credits. Climbing into the brown leather desk chair behind my desk, I picked up my light blue backpack from the floor. I pulled out a floral-patterned ring-bound calendar to see what the day would bring.

Opening my calendar to today's page, a yellow sticky note stuck to the center read,

"Have a great day, honey. Love you."

It was from Joe Weatherton, my boyfriend. He must have snuck it into my calendar. My cheeks rose as a big smile formed on my face. I pulled the note from the page and moved it to the inside back cover.

Turning back to the calendar page for June 16th, I saw we would be working on chapter 3 of *Into the Wild* for senior English. I was excited to use this book in class as it was one of my favorites.

After taking a deep breath, I walked to the back of the room to get a copy of the book. I was so glad that Joe worked with multiple schools in the area as the school resource officer. It helped us to borrow copies of this book from Mulston High School instead of having to purchase them, otherwise I would have had to select something else due to a tight summer school budget. As I pulled the book from the shelf, a folded piece of lined notebook paper came with it. Picking it up from the floor, I unfolded the paper and started reading. It was a letter.

Dear Mom,

I am so sorry to disappoint you. I know you were upset when the police came and told you I was bullying someone at school. I wish you could understand why I felt I had to do it.

When I was taken off the varsity baseball team at Mulston High, I now know it was because of the prank I pulled. But, when I saw my teammate Caleb talking with the ASU baseball coach, I thought I was losing my place on that team too.

I found out later that Caleb had already been talking to ASU about playing for them and had a spot. He was meeting with them to confirm it by signing his letter of intent. Had I known that, it may have stopped me from making his brother Shawn a target of my anger.

It makes it even harder to confess what I did because you and Dad are friends with the Townsons from seeing them at all the Manor City summer baseball games.

Do you want to know what I did? I started by meeting him at the bike racks and giving him a hard time. I convinced myself that I was just teasing him. Then I typed up notes on my computer and put them in his locker. And I asked my friends to do it too, in case others had seen me do it.

I felt pretty good getting my anger out this way. Caleb even talked to me about picking on Shawn just after Thanksgiving. I told him I would let up, but I didn't.

Then I came up with the big idea: post something on The Bulldog about Shawn liking to look at naked guys. I thought this was funny. Well, Shawn didn't. He almost killed himself over it.

So, the fact that I must complete anger management counseling and will have to work extra hard for a spot on the college baseball team is my fault. It has nothing to do with you or Dad.

As I am sitting with my counselor, I am writing this letter to help me deal with my anger issues.

Josh

I looked up from the letter and gazed out of the window. The only Josh I knew of was a student at Mulston High School who had targeted my boyfriend's nephew, Shawn. The letter does mention the Townsons, which is their last name. *I wonder how the letter got here?* And after reading his words, I became more interested in Josh's story and why he chose to make Shawn a target.

As a teacher, I have seen many interactions between students. The ones who bully typically hide their behavior from teachers and school administrators because they don't want to get in trouble. Kind of like how teens hide their behavior from their parents. When other teens see one of their classmates harassing someone, they typically won't stop the behavior for fear of retaliation—by the one who bullies or their friends.

I got to know Shawn through family events I attended with Joe. Shawn is a bright, funny, but shy teen. I also noticed Shawn was caught in his brother's shadow, which pulled him one step out of the view of everyone else. This isolated Shawn from his parents as Caleb received most of their attention. It also kept them from noticing the signs that something was wrong.

After school, I met Joe for dinner at his house and told him about the letter.

"You just found that in one of the books?" Joe asked, as he was drying his hands with the dish towel.

"Yes. He must have turned the book in and forgot it was in there. The books did come from Mulston and that is where he went to school."

"It makes sense," Joe replied. He grabbed the pepper grinder off the counter to season the chicken.

"Joe, what would you think about me talking to Josh about what happened?" I asked. Sitting at the kitchen island, I took a sip of ice water from my glass.

"What do you mean?"

"How would you feel about me talking to Josh about what happened? Why he chose to make Shawn a target. I think it may help to hear the other side of what happened."

"Help who?"

It was a fair question. "Help me to understand the full story about what happened, and for Josh to tell his side," I replied. I got down from the swivel stool and headed toward the refrigerator.

"Monica...I have learned a lot through the bullying workshops I've attended as a school resource officer and a cop. That isn't how these things are typically handled."

"I know, Joe, but it may help him to cope with what's happened." Reaching into the refrigerator, I poured more water from the pitcher into my glass. "It may also help to bring the families together."

"I don't know..." Joe hesitated.

"I think we should try it," I said.

"You can, but only if he is willing to. He's eighteen, so technically you wouldn't have to have his parents' consent, but you may want to ask them how they feel about it."

"Of course."

I know there is something to be learned from having both sides of a story of one who bullies and his target. I was glad that Joe was supportive of me looking into this.

SELMA P. VERDE

Let me tell you a little bit about Josh and his backstory…

JOSH'S STORY

Josh's story begins as an only child in an upper-class family. His dad, William Alberts, is a very well-known trial lawyer in the area, and his mom, Caroline, is William's very supportive wife. Josh was brought up lacking for nothing and was working toward becoming a professional baseball player. This wasn't something his parents just put him into. He had natural talent for the game and was busy playing it while his parents were busy with parent things.

Don't get me wrong, he loves to play baseball, but also wanted attention from his parents. He was starting to get bored, not with baseball, but with home. So, what did he do? He started to damage things around the house, starting with a vase his mom picked up in Italy. When she saw it was broken, she thought one of the cleaning people must have done it and yelled at them. Then he damaged the garage door with a bat. That time, his dad knew it was him, but instead of punishing Josh for it, he just yelled at Josh and had the garage door fixed.

When the little things weren't getting their attention, he started getting into bigger trouble. Spray-painting sides of buildings, setting fire to garbage cans, and destroying benches at the park. Josh would get picked up by the police, arrested, and his dad, being a big-time lawyer, would bail him out of trouble so nothing would hit his record. The son of the most well-known attorney can't have a criminal record. Nor can an up-and-coming baseball star on his way to going pro.

The Big Prank

The summer before Josh's junior year at Mulston High, he and some friends decided to build a stunner, a device used in Tangorka, a popular online game that teens played with each other, to stun your enemies so you could get past them and onto the next levels. They decided to set a replica they built under the bleachers at the Brooklyn Heights homecoming game. When they planned it, they thought it would be just a prank. They thought it might create a little damage to the bleachers, but never thought it would do the extent of damage it did, even injuring two people as they tried to get off the bleachers. It is what got Josh and his friends into big trouble and landed them into juvenile detention.

Josh hoped his parents would bail him out again, as they had always done in the past. Since the law really got involved this time, it was too much for his dad to have to pay off and not be noticed for doing so. So, William decided this would be a good time to let Josh feel the consequences of his actions.

The Consequences

During his time at Creekside—almost a full year—Josh kept up with his studies so he could start his senior year in the fall, but he did lose something very important to him: his spot on the Mulston High School varsity baseball team. Playing on the team in his senior year would help him to claim his spot on the college team at ASU and continue his path to becoming a professional player. Because of the prank, though, he was pulled from the team and would have to try to pursue his dream of playing professional baseball some other way.

Josh was disappointed, to say the least, and on top of that he thought one of his teammates, Caleb Townson, had taken his place on the college team. Josh assumed that was the end of his journey to professional baseball and was mad about it. So mad, he wanted to get back at Caleb. Josh decided to pick on Shawn, Caleb's brother, to get back at him.

Talking to Josh about His Side

After reading Josh's letter and learning more about his background, I really wanted to talk to him about what happened. It would also give me a chance to give Josh his letter back. My first step was to call Josh to see if he would talk about what happened. He answered after the second ring.

"Hello."

"Hi Josh, my name is Monica Freberg. I'm a teacher at Brooklyn Heights. I wanted to talk to you about the situation you had with Shawn Townson."

"Why do you want to talk to me?"

"I am interested to hear your side of things."

"Really? No one's asked me to talk about it like this before. So far, everyone's been seeing me as a bad person, and either ignore me or call me names."

"I don't see it that way."

"I don't know if it's a good idea. I don't want to get into more trouble."

"I am not a cop or member of law enforcement. Our conversation would have nothing to do with the consequences of what you did. That has already been decided by the school. I just want to know what happened from your side of things."

"Okay. I'll meet with you."

"Thank you, Josh. How about Thursday afternoon. Say about three thirty? Do you know where the Rise and Perk is over by the community center?"

"That works for me. I know where the Rise and Perk is. I'll come after my therapy appointment."

"I look forward to seeing you then."

I was so glad he wanted to share what happened with me. *I hope I can give him a chance to feel heard.*

When I arrived at the Rise and Perk coffee shop, I went to the counter and ordered a chai tea latte. As I looked out the window, I saw Josh sitting at a table, shifting in his seat, appearing anxious. Normal reaction to have before a talk like this. I walked up to the table.

"Hi Josh. How are you doing?" I asked.

"Ah, okay."

"Just okay?"

"Yeah."

I sat down across from him. After setting my backpack on the floor, I reached into it and brought out a folded piece of paper and handed it to Josh. "Here is your letter. I found it in one of the copies of *Into the Wild*."

"I was wondering where that letter went. It was one I wrote during one of my therapy sessions with Dr. Benson."

"Are you planning on giving it to your mom?"

"I'm not sure."

"Okay. Do you want to talk about what happened?"

"I do. It's a little bit hard for me, though."

"I understand. I want you to try and be as open as you can with me so we can help you understand how you are feeling."

"Okay."

"Let's start with how you are feeling right now?"

"I thought I would feel better about doing this. I don't really want to be here now."

"Why is that?"

"What if it's a waste of everyone's time? Everyone knows what I've done, why do we need to talk about it?"

"There are two sides to every story, and I want to hear yours."

"No one cares about my side. I'm just seen as the one who bullies. The mean one."

"I care about your side, Josh. Why did you decide to pick on Shawn?"

"Because I thought Caleb took my place on the team. I felt like someone needed to pay me back for not being able to pursue baseball the way I had planned. I knew I couldn't go after Caleb as that would not help me get back on track. I was mad at him, too. Then I remember seeing Shawn, his younger brother, leave freshmen orientation the day I picked up my schedule and talked to Coach Kraft. I thought, maybe it would make me feel better to hassle him a bit."

"Why not pick on Caleb? He's the one you thought took your spot."

"I thought I may have had a chance to win my spot back. Picking on a teammate wouldn't have gone over very well."

"I see. So how did it feel to pick on Shawn?"

"At first, it made me feel good to release my anger and make someone pay. I wasn't planning on hassling him for very long. But it turned out to be more gratifying for me than I thought. It made me feel better because I felt like someone was paying for my bad luck. But after a while, it got boring. Shawn was an easy target."

"Easy?"

"Yeah. He didn't fight back. He just took it and ran and hid with his friend Bae Kwon."

"So, Bae also knew you were making Shawn a target?"

"I guess so. He was always hanging around with Shawn when I saw him."

"Did you bully Bae also?"

"No, I just picked on Shawn."

"So how did Marzon Jacobs get involved?"

"I asked him to help me put some of the notes in Shawn's locker."

"Is that all he did?"

"Directly, yes."

"What does that mean?"

"Well, he got into trouble with his username on The Bulldog."

"The Bulldog?"

"Yeah, that's the Mulston online student forum."

"What did he do?"

"They found out his username was the one who sent a friend request and messages to Shawn."

"Why isn't he in trouble like you are, then?"

"*I* used his username to send the messages."

"How did you get a hold of his login credentials?"

"I stole them from his gym locker. We played a game of pick-up basketball, and I said I would meet him in the gym, and I got into his locker and got the information to set up his profile."

"Why did you set up Marzon's profile for him?" I asked. "Wasn't he planning on setting it up?"

"No. Marzon didn't care about The Bulldog. So, I took his credentials so Shawn wouldn't know it was me harassing him."

"Oh, I see. Tell me about getting access to The Bulldog intranet."

"I set up Marzon's profile from the instructions that came with the login information."

"And you weren't worried about getting Marzon in trouble for what you were doing?"

"I figured he would be okay with me just using his since he didn't really care about being on it anyway. It was only going to be a little bit of teasing."

"But it became a little more than that, right?" I sipped at my chai tea latte as I listened.

"I kept getting madder and madder about what happened. I started working out with the town team to get my baseball back on track and they were giving me a hard time about what I did and so I quit. My quitting that team would probably keep me from going any further in baseball. So, I wanted to take a big stab Shawn."

"What did you do?"

"I posted on The Bulldog that Shawn likes looking at naked guys in the locker room."

"And what was that supposed to do?"

"Make all the guys think he was weird and not want to hang around him."

I tilted my head. "Do you know how Shawn reacted to that?"

"Yeah, he tried to kill himself," Josh admitted.

"He became petrified of what everyone was going to say to him after spring break. Then, he attempted to hang himself."

"What?"

"Yes, Josh, he attempted to hang himself over what you posted on The Bulldog."

There was a pause in the conversation. Josh looked down at the table. An uncomfortable silence took over as he took a sip of his coffee.

Josh looked at me. "He must have been upset about more than just that. I was just teasing him."

I shook my head. "That isn't how Shawn took it. It was the final straw after all the harassment you'd been doing to him."

"Come on. He needs to get tougher skin."

"Josh, do you realize you were making Shawn a target of bullying? And that you were the one who bullies?"

"I am not a bully. I answered yes to a few of those questions at the Go Blue presentation at school, but that doesn't make me a bully."

"Josh, you were acting like one in how you were treating Shawn. And it almost killed him."

"That must be why Caleb came and talked to me."

"What did Caleb say to you?"

Josh recalled the events, relaying them to us:

"Townson. What are you doing by my car?"
"I need to talk to you about my brother Shawn."

"What about him?"

"The fact that you made him feel so bad that he felt the only way out was to try and kill himself."

"You have no proof it was me, Caleb."

"Oh, but I do. My brother told me you were giving him a hard time. I even told you to stop and you just kept on doing it."

"I can't help it that your brother is so sensitive."

"You wouldn't let up on him, Josh. You just kept doing it and doing it until he couldn't take it. Aren't you even sorry about it?"

"I was just giving him a hard time. Not my fault he couldn't take it."

"Josh, I have known you since we played tee-ball together. I never thought you would get this mad about not being on a team. You are a good player, but you are a sore loser. And you are taking it out on someone else. I'm planning on making a report to the police about you, Josh."

"So, you are going to become a tattler now, Caleb?"

"No. I'm doing what is right. And I should have done it when Shawn first told me. Instead of trying to talk to you and get you to stop. I thought you would hear what I had to say. I guess I was wrong."

"Why do you think Caleb took the time to confront you about what you did?" I asked Josh.

"Because I was giving his brother a hard time and he almost died."

I nodded. "Seems like you were only seeing things your way. You didn't see the effect you were having on Shawn."

"I know it wasn't the right thing to do."

"It's great that you realize what you did was wrong. But it doesn't make what you did all right now. You cannot take your anger out on other people. Your not making the ASU baseball team was the consequence of something you did. It had nothing to do with Shawn."

"No, I know it didn't. But I wanted to get back at Caleb for taking my place at ASU."

"Why were you convinced that Caleb took your place? He plays shortstop and you play first base, right?"

"Yeah, but I thought they may only take so many

freshmen players and that spot wasn't going to be available for me if Caleb had it."

"How did you know if Caleb was committing to play at ASU?"

"I saw him talking with the ASU coach and Coach Kraft in the conference room, and Caleb was signing a form."

"So, you assumed. Did you ever ask the coach or Caleb about it?"

"No." Josh's gaze fell to his coffee. He let out a big sigh and his eyes began to well with tears. "Why did I feel I needed to do that to Shawn? Why was I so mad at Caleb?"

"You tell me, Josh."

"I have worked hard my entire life to make it in baseball. My parents have enough money to send me to college without the scholarship. But I had earned a place on the college team. I felt my opportunity slipping away and was convinced it was Caleb's fault."

"Why did you bring Shawn into it?"

"If I started harassing Caleb, the team would find out that I was jealous of Caleb. Shawn was an easier target."

"Do you think Caleb would have fought back?"

"Caleb wouldn't have let me harass him. He would have told me to get lost and get over the fact that I wasn't going to make the college team based on what I did at the Brooklyn Heights homecoming game."

"Would you have left it alone?" I asked. "Gotten over it?"

"I'm not sure. I probably would've still been mad and taken my anger out somewhere else."

I took another long, thoughtful sip of my latte. "So, did you get what you wanted out of harassing Shawn?"

"What do you mean?"

"Did it make you feel better about not making the team?"

"No," confessed Josh.

"Then how did it make you feel?" I asked.

"I lost control of my baseball career, so making Shawn a target of my anger made me feel powerful over something."

"Was that fair to Shawn?"

"No. But I felt the need for someone to pay for my lost opportunity. And that someone was Shawn."

"How do you feel now?"

"Terrible for Shawn for the fact he almost killed himself over what happened to me. And terrible for me, because I couldn't handle the consequences of what I did."

"Why did you struggle so hard with taking responsibility for what happened at the football game?"

"I guess because I never had to take responsibility before. My dad always bailed me out of trouble. I was mad at my parents for the fact I was at Creekside and let that get in the way of dealing with the consequences of what I did. It also made things harder on me while I was serving my time."

"How so?"

"Because I was so mad, I wouldn't cooperate with the counselors at Creekside. So, I spent a lot of time in solitary confinement."

"What did you do while in solitary?"

"Did a lot of thinking about how I got there and what I would need to do to get out. I was also working on my homework so I could stay caught up and graduate on time to go onto ASU."

"Are you going to graduate on time?" I wondered.

"I have three classes left to finish. I'll have to do them in summer school."

"Have you been able to play any baseball?"

"I'm on the B squad of the town team, the Manor City Orioles. They took me back after I quit last fall. I will probably never play college baseball and if I am going to make the major leagues, I will have to play through the minor league system first. It's a longer road than going straight through to college."

I nodded encouragingly. "You are a good person, Josh. You just made some bad choices that put you on a path of bad behavior."

"Looking back, it wasn't the right thing to do. And it got me into a lot of trouble when the school found out I was making Shawn Townson a target."

"This talk is a great start working on yourself and your feelings about what happened. How would you feel about talking to Shawn about it?" I asked, feeling like it would be a good next step.

"It will be hard for me to do. I know the Townsons," Josh replied. "Can I think about it?"

"Sure. I'll need to know soon so we can keep the process going. Whether you decide to talk to them or not, I recommend sitting down and writing a letter like the one you did for your mom. It will help you sort out what you want to say and help organize the facts about what happened."

"I'll let you know. Is our talk over now?"

"For now. I look forward to hearing from you."

"Thank you."

"You're welcome, Josh." I smiled at him as I stood. "Thank you, for being willing to talk to me."

As I heard more and more about what happened to Shawn, from his side and Josh's, I became more aware of how deep the effects of bullying can go. Shawn had been just steps away from killing himself over it. He'd felt there was no other way out. No one seemed to be listening and all the attention had been on Caleb.

It confirmed the idea I had while talking to Josh and I wanted to run it by Joe as we were sitting down to have dessert.

"What would you think about bringing Shawn and Josh together to talk about it?" I asked Joe, taking a small bite of cheesecake.

Joe set his fork down on the table. "Why?" he asked.

"I think it may help both of them to hear the other side of what happened."

Joe looked at me sidelong. "Do you really think it will help them?" he asked. "Or is it more your own curiosity?"

Again, it was a fair question. "These two know each other, Joe. It may help both to cope with what happened, but it may also help to bring the families together. We could even ask Dr. Gallagher to be there to lend some professional direction if needed." I was thinking it could help to bring in Shawn's psychologist who started with him after the suicide attempt. Of course, Joe could be there, too. As a cop, he could be a mediator and deescalate the situation if needed.

"I don't know, Monica…"

"I think we should try it."

"Only if all parties are willing to," he conceded.

"Of course."

Now I would need to talk to both parties and see if they would be willing to meet.

Next Steps

I think about Josh's story and what his path to becoming one who bullies looks like. I learned it isn't a story of one who sets out to be mean just for the sake of it. That was his reaction to what happened to him. It wasn't right, but without having learned how to cope with consequences, and without his parents engaged in his life, he didn't know of a better way to process how he felt.

Many stories about people who bully are just like Josh's. Sometimes, a person who bullies is suffering from mental illness or has been the victim of abuse at home. That isn't what Josh was dealing with in this case.

I called Josh's parents and asked them if I could talk to them about what happened. I needed to continue to learn more and possibly help Josh and Shawn.

The file with Josh's parents' contact information was in my backpack. I walked into the bedroom to get it and then dialed the number. The call was answered after the second ring.

"Hello, this is Caroline."

"Hello, my name is Monica Freberg. I'm a teacher at Brooklyn Heights. I was wondering if I can get together with you and your husband and discuss the incident that occurred between your son Josh and another student, Shawn Townson."

"Well, Monica, I am not sure what we would accomplish by doing that. Josh is required to talk to a counselor to determine further direction. So, he is working on making things better."

"Caroline, I think it could help everyone to understand what happened and talk out their feelings about it. You and your husband must have your own thoughts about what happened, and those thoughts may be helpful to share with Josh. I am also interested in learning more about Josh's side of things to complete the story of what happened."

"I am not sure how my husband will feel about it. He doesn't have a lot of spare time as he is busy with cases right now. Didn't you already talk to Josh?"

"Yes, I did, but I think it's important for us to take the time to help both Josh and Shawn process what happened. You and your husband may want to make time to talk about this."

"You know, I had no idea that Josh was targeting Shawn until the police showed up at my door," Caroline told me. "The situation was bad but could have been a lot worse. There is no excuse for what Josh did, but my husband and I should have been more involved in our son's life, for many reasons other than maybe preventing bullying from happening at all."

"I am not trying to question what you did," I assured her. "I'd like for both Josh and Shawn to have time and a safe place to discuss what happened."

"Okay. I will talk to my husband and see what he has to say. I will call you back."

Joe and I decided the best way to talk to Shawn's parents—Jessica and Steve, Joe's sister—as well as try to get Shawn's response to what happened, would be to meet up at their house. After having a great dinner from the grill, we sat down to talk with Steve, Jessica, and Shawn.

"You know, I had no idea that Josh was targeting Shawn until we got the call when we got off the airplane in Arizona," Jessica started. "We were told that Shawn had tried to kill himself because he was being bullied at school. The situation was bad but could have been a lot worse. There is no excuse for what Josh did, but Steve and I should have been more involved in our son's life."

"Shawn is required to talk to a counselor," Steve added, "not only to help him deal with what happened, but also to help us work on things as a family. After talking to Dr. Gallagher about this, she seemed to think a talk between Shawn and Josh could be a good idea, as long as both sides were willing to do it."

"Shawn, do you want to talk to Josh about what he did to you?" Joe asked his nephew.

"Do I have to?" Shawn said.

Jessica reached out to grab Shawn's hand. "No, honey, you don't."

"But it would probably help you and Josh process your feelings about what happened," Joe said, "and it would help to bring the families together."

Steve said, "We weren't really close to the Alberts, but it would be nice to clear the air."

Getting Josh on Board with the Talk

After our meeting with the Townsons, I reached out to Josh to see what he thought about the idea.

"The talk we had the other day is a great start to working on yourself and your feelings about what happened. Remember when we talked about the next step being a meeting with Shawn and his parents to help Shawn process what has happened and work on his feelings? We asked if he was willing to talk to you and he said yes. Would you be willing to talk to him, Josh?"

"It will be hard for me to do. I know the Townsons. Will Caleb be there?"

"Probably not since this didn't happen directly to him. The conversation is really between you and Shawn, but Shawn may want his parents to be there. You can have your parents at the session if you would like."

"Can I think about it?"

"Sure."

Josh called me back two days later. He said he would like to clear the air with Shawn and the Townsons. I asked him if his parents would be attending, and he said no. I contacted all parties involved and reserved the conference room at the community center the following Saturday.

Joe and I arrived an hour early to set up.

"It will be interesting to see how this goes," Joe said as he unlocked the conference room door.

"There is something to be learned from both sides of each story of one who bullies and his or her target. Both sides are hurt by what happens."

"That is true. It's great that you were able to get both sides together to talk about this, honey. I'm proud of you."

"Thank you, Joe. But this conversation is not about me at all. It's about two people and their families learning about the other side of what happened to them."

Josh arrived first, then Jessica, Steve, and finally, Shawn Townson. The Townsons went into the conference room while Josh remained out in the hallway, leaning against the wall. Just before the meeting time, Joe met with Josh and urged him to come into the conference room.

Shawn and his parents were already seated in the room. I walked in with a pot of coffee and set it down on a tray, stocked with cream and sugar, in the center of the table, next to a box of tissues.

Steve Townson looked up at Josh as he walked in with Joe. He shook his head, then smiled.

"Hey, Josh," Steve greeted.

Josh cleared his throat. "Hello, Mr. Townson." He took a seat next to Joe opposite of the Townsons.

I took my place at the table. "Thank you all for being here. I know this isn't an easy conversation. I have talked to both Josh and Shawn and think they are ready to discuss what happened and maybe get a better understanding of how the other one felt and dealt with the situation."

Expectant faces looked back at me. Jessica, Shawn's mom, poured herself a cup of coffee.

I continued, "Steve and Jessica, I would ask that you just listen to what Josh and Shawn have to say and try not to interject your feelings or thoughts. I would like to see how Josh and Shawn are feeling as they express their side of the story."

Steve and Jessica traded a look, then both nodded in agreement.

"Thank you." I smiled. "Josh, do you want to speak first?"

"Sure." Josh looked over at Shawn. Peering back at Josh, Shawn shifted in his chair, looking less than comfortable.

Josh said, "I have thought a lot about what I would say to you, Shawn. I have seen you grow from a little tagalong brother of Caleb's into a freshman at Mulston." He paused. "This is harder than I thought it would be."

"Take your time," I encouraged.

Josh swallowed. "When I heard that I wasn't going to be able to play varsity baseball my senior year, I was mad. I thought about it for a while, decided I was good enough and could still get where I wanted to go. I would show everyone that I could. I went to talk to Coach Kraft and tell him I planned to still play baseball, then I saw Caleb in the conference room talking to the ASU coach. I thought it meant my chance to play ball at ASU was gone. That was something I had worked for through all those years of playing baseball in the Manor City leagues. I could hardly stand waiting for Coach Kraft after that, so I left."

"Then what happened?" I asked.

"I went home and thought about everything and decided I needed to do something to get rid of all my anger and get back at Caleb."

Steve and Jessica gasped at Josh's response. Jessica opened her mouth to speak, but I slid her a look. She conceded with a sigh, bringing her coffee mug to her lips.

I asked Josh, "Why did you feel it was Caleb's fault?"

"It was my initial reaction to what I saw. I didn't think it all through logically at the time. I just saw it as Caleb took my place."

"So how does Shawn become involved?"

"I knew if I went after Caleb, the coach and the team wouldn't ever support me trying to get back into baseball. It would be too public. So, I did the next thing I could think of, and decided to go after his younger brother. It is normal for seniors to pick on freshmen, so it made sense to me."

"So, you just started picking on Shawn?"

"It was just teasing. I put notes in his locker and hassled him at the bike racks. Nothing that a senior wouldn't do to a freshman."

"So, you saw it more as hazing than bullying?"

"Yes. Like a rite of passage to become one of the big kids at school."

"But that isn't how Shawn saw it, was it, Shawn?"

"No," Shawn said. "I didn't know why you wanted to pick on me, Josh."

"Did you see it as teasing, Shawn?" I asked, hoping to keep Shawn talking.

"It really hurt my feelings that a friend of Caleb's was being so mean to me."

"Did you tell Caleb about it?"

"Yes, I did. He talked to Josh, but it didn't do any good."

"Josh, why didn't you stop when Caleb asked you to?" I wondered.

"I was mad at him for taking my place. I definitely wasn't going to let him tell me what to do."

"And this continued through winter break, all the way up until spring break, right?"

"Yes," Josh said honestly.

"Then your post on The Bulldog showed up under Marzon's username."

"Yeah."

"Shawn, where were you during spring break?"

"I was staying with my grandma while my parents and Caleb were out of town."

"Why did you post it, Josh?"

"To get his attention and be funny."

"It didn't come off as funny, did it?"

"No," he admitted.

I looked at Shawn. "How did you feel when you read his post on The Bulldog?"

Shawn sat back in his chair and clenched his fists. His eyes started to well up with tears. He took a deep, fortifying breath then spoke up again.

"I was alone in the spare bedroom of my grandma's house when I read it. I knew the whole school would see it too. How could I show myself at school again after that? So, I went up into the attic and tried to kill myself at my grandma's house."

The room fell silent.

"How does hearing that make you feel, Josh?" I asked quietly. "That he wanted to kill himself over something you posted on the school intranet?"

"At the time, I thought he was overreacting. I was trying to be funny. But after talking to you about my actions, and seeing Shawn now, I know it was a big mistake and the wrong thing to do."

"You almost didn't get to see Shawn now, Josh. How does that make you feel?"

"Not so good. He is a teammate and friend of mine's brother. I should never have taken my anger out on him." Josh turned to look directly at Shawn, remorse in his eyes. "I'm sorry, Shawn."

Jessica and Steve reached out to put their hands on Shawn's shoulders. Shawn still had tears in his eyes when he met Josh's gaze. I took a sip of water and continued the conversation.

"I was with Shawn at the hospital when he told me it was you who was making him a target. Shawn and I have also been talking through his thoughts and feelings about what has happened ever since. He's had some tough things to deal with because of this. Shawn, do you want to share?"

Shawn's eyes were glossy with tears. I slid the tissue box over to him. "We can take a little break if you want to," I said.

"No, I'm good." After drying his eyes, Shawn sat up straighter in his chair and took a deep breath, then spoke. "I felt so lost, I didn't know what to do. Someone was harassing me and wouldn't stop no matter how much I asked. I didn't know what I did to deserve being his target."

"I was mad about not being allowed back on the team,"

Josh said, sorrowfully. "That was my fault, and I shouldn't have taken it out on you."

"Why did you then?" Shawn asked.

"To get back at Caleb. I thought he had taken my spot."

"But he didn't, right? He earned his spot."

"Yeah, he did. I didn't know that then. Still, it was no excuse for doing what I did to you."

The room was quiet again. After a moment, I said, "I think that's a good place to stop for today. It's going to take a while to sort all these feelings out. Shawn will continue to see Dr. Gallagher as he comes into his sophomore year at Mulston. Josh will work with Dr. Benson for anger management and to discuss what his next steps will be. I am so glad the two of you started the conversation today." I wasn't sure what would happen next, but I hoped it would eventually lead to healing—for both of them.

"Thank you for bringing the kids together to talk about this, Monica," Jessica said. "Hopefully they can both walk away with a little better understanding of what the other one went through." She looked over at her husband, a soft smile on her face. "It helps us understand a little better, too."

"You're welcome, Jessica. And thank you, all of you, for your willingness to be here. I wish more people were able to come together and have both sides talk like this. Understanding each perspective in these situations may be a way to put a stop to them."

"I bet you're right," Steve said. "Thank you, again."

As they left and we started to pack up, Joe spoke for the first time since the meeting began. "I know you don't want to give yourself credit, but that took a lot of courage, honey."

I smiled at Joe. "Thank you, but they are the brave ones. That couldn't have been easy for either of them."

"Very true." And he gave me a kiss.

Find out more about what happened to Shawn by reading the teen novel *Shawn's Way*, book two of *The Way Series*.

IN CONCLUSION

Through this short story, I wanted to illustrate that Josh isn't just some mean kid. He had everything going for him and due to some bad decisions, all those good things disappeared. Too few stories exist about the one who bullies. If we can understand their situation better, their perspective, we can help put an end to bullying. This concept of bringing both parties together to talk afterward is one idea that may help both the one who bullies, and the target, or the one who is bullied, understand each other. If they can be open to talking about what is wrong, it ultimately may help both sides feel compassion toward one another.

We don't often get to see the target and the one who bullies come together to discuss candidly what happened. It wasn't an easy thing for either Josh or Shawn to do. It might have been made easier by the fact that Josh and Shawn knew each other through Caleb and there was some vested interest due to the families knowing each other. But in many cases, the target is so afraid of the one who bullies that they would probably not agree to confronting them or are not around to do so.

I wrote "Josh's Story" to illustrate one option for how to start tackling the problem of bullying. This session not only helped Josh to better understand what he did, but it opened communication between him and Shawn.

What did we learn from this story?

Shawn's Way and "Josh's Story" illustrate two sides of a typical bullying situation.

The people involved knew each other through at least one mutual connection. In this case, that mutual connection was Caleb Townson.

Bullying is never the right thing to do. One should never pick on or harass another person, regardless of how they may feel about something.

Could this situation have been avoided? Yes. Josh made an assumption that turned out to not be true. Perhaps he made this assumption because he *wanted* it to be true. Caleb wasn't taking his spot on the ASU baseball team; Caleb had his own spot. Josh lost his spot by his own doing. It was the consequence of the prank he and his friends had pulled at the Brooklyn Heights homecoming game. Had Josh accepted that responsibility, or had his parents done more to equip him with healthy ways to handle that disappointment, he could have focused his attention on trying to get into collegiate-level baseball in an alternative way.

In both cases, the parents had no idea this was happening. Take the time to engage with your teenagers and give them a safe place to come and talk to you about what is happening in their lives. In this case, since the families know each other, they may have been able to sort the issue out before Shawn attempted suicide.

Resources

This is a story about a teenager who bullies.

There are two sides in every instance of bullying. A person

who bullies is never "right" in making someone a target, but there is often more to the story than someone bullying someone else just to be mean. They likely have a deeper, perhaps uninvestigated reason for their acting-out. These reasons *never* justify their decision to bully, but understanding them may help even them to see that they need to talk to someone about what they are feeling and experiencing, and get help unpacking those emotions. Recognizing the side of the one who bullies can often help others understand why it is happening, so that they can work to put a stop to it.

There are things we can do to help a person who bullies and their targets. Mentoring A Dream has a resource that lists out the following ideas.

How can we help those who bully others?

Acknowledge their behavior and ask them, "Did you hurt anyone?" Or, "Would you want someone to treat you that way?"

Give yourself some time to process what is happening before reacting.

Help them think through their actions and help them understand the consequences.

Be proactive in making the situation right with the party they set up as a target.

How can we help the targets?

Reassure them that what is happening is not their fault.

Give yourself some time to process what is happening before reacting.

Check in with them and see how they are doing. Suggest that they talk to someone who can help them process and can report what is happening to them.

Find a resource that will help them work through their

feelings and be able to start the reporting process to stop the one who bullies.

Quoted from the Mentoring A Dream – Bullying Resource

If you are being bullied or think suicide may be the only way out, please reach out to one of these resources for help:

STOP BULLYING NOW HOTLINE (USA)
1-800-273-8255 (TALK)
www.stopbullying.gov/resources/get-help-now

National Suicide Prevention Lifeline
1-800-273-8255 (TALK)
www.SuicidePreventionLifeline.org

ABOUT THE AUTHOR

Selma P. Verde has been a creative writer since she was a kid, starting with silly plays and creative storytelling. It was her dream as a teenager to write and publish a novel. As an adult, watching the kids around her growing up and learning life's lessons inspired her to write about some of the challenges teenagers face. Those are the themes she focuses on in her coming-of-age novels for the teen and young adult audiences. Selma lives in Minnesota with the man in her life, Jim, his two sons Max and Mitch, their cat Sophie, and their dog Philo.

Be sure to check out her website, www.selmapverde.com or follow her on social media:

Facebook: https://www.facebook.com/selmapverde
Pinterest: https://www.pinterest.com/selmapverde/
Instagram: @selmapverde
Twitter: @selmapverde

Contact Selma: https://selmapverde.com/contact/

www.ingramcontent.com/pod-product-compliance
Lightning Source LLC
Chambersburg PA
CBHW060956120626
46557CB00003B/1192